P9-CDC-627

Probity Jones and the Fear Not Angel

Written by
Walter Wangerin, Jr.

Illustrated by
Tim Ladwig

PARACLETE PRESS
BREWSTER, MASSACHUSETTS

To my dear godchildren,
Tiffany Rouse and Brandon Piper;
both of whom have been to the pageant,
bright, shining like the angels

Probity Jones and the Fear Not Angel

2005 First Paraclete Press Edition

ISBN 1-55725-457-5

Library of Congress Cataloging-in-Publication Data
Wangerin, Walter.
Probity Jones and the Fear Not Angel / written by Walter Wangerin, Jr. ; illustrated by Tim Ladwig.
p. cm.
Summary: When she misses the Christmas pageant because she is sick, a young African American girl is visited by an angel who takes her back to witness the first Christmas.
ISBN 1-55725-457-5
[1. Christmas—Fiction. 2. Angels—Fiction. 3. African Americans—Fiction. 4. Jesus Christ—Nativity—Fiction.] I. Ladwig, Tim, ill. II. Title.
PZ7.W1814Pr 2005
[Fic]—dc22 2005048661

Published by Paraclete Press
Brewster, Massachusetts
www.paracletepress.com

10 9 8 7 6 5 4 3 2 1

Printed in Singapore

The whole family was getting dressed to go out—everyone except Probity. Probity Jones was sick. Her mother had told her she was too sick to leave the apartment tonight.

"I'm sorry child," her mother had said. "You're burnin' with fever, and it's colder than zero outside."

"Oh, Mama, I *got* to go," Probity begged, trying to sit up. "I been plannin' this for weeks. I memorized all the words. I can say them perfectly. Please, Mama—please let me go with you."

Then her mother heaved a sorrowful sigh. It was the kind of sigh that always made Probity feel bad. Her mother was worn out from working, worn out from taking care of her four children alone, worn out from being forever and ever poor. How could Probity argue with such a sigh?

"Baby," her mother said, "when I lost your daddy to sickness, I promised God I'd never lose another soul. I'm keeping the family whole, and you are staying home tonight."

So that was final.

And now Probity could hear her sisters laughing in the kitchen.

"Snip-snip! Snip-snip!" That was Elfrieda. "Snip the tinfoil, make a star, and cover it over with glitter!"

Probity lay on the sofa in the front room. It was dark outside. Probity was watching the white moon through the window. It shined on the snowy tops of the evergreen trees, but it moved all alone in heaven. Probity thought, *The moon is as lonely as I am.*

Just then her little brother started to yell, "Where's my baffrobe? Who stole my baffrobe? I can't go without my baffrobe, you know!"

Elfrieda said, "Go ask Probity. Girls who lose expensive coats are liable to steal bathrobes too."

The kitchen door burst open. Light rushed into the front room. So did Probity's brother with his lip stuck out.

"Probity!" He marched to the sofa and gave her a punch on the shoulder. "Did you steal my baffrobe to wear to church tonight on account of you lost your own coat?"

"No, Charles." Probity felt like crying. "I don't have your bathrobe, and I'm not going with you tonight."

Charles' eyes grew large. "Why not?" he said. He grabbed his sister's nightgown. "Probity, you *got* to go!"

"I can't," she said.

" 'Cause you lost your coat? 'Cause Mama's mad at you? You can wear my baffrobe. I don't mind."

"No, Charles. It's because I'm sick."

Her little brother got tears in his eyes. "But I'm scared without you, Probe," he said. "You and me, we're supposed to say the words *together*. How can I say the words without you?"

Probity touched his cheek and said, "Say them now."

Charles frowned. He said, "Let us go—" He paused and frowned harder. "Let us go now— Let us now go—" Then he wailed, "Oh, Probity, I don't know it. I can't say it without you!"

"Shhh," said Probity, "Listen to me: *Let us now go even unto Bethlehem—*"

But Charles only howled louder and tried to pull his sister off the sofa. "I need you, Probe. I really need you!"

Then their mother came into the room with a wrinkled cotton bathrobe. "Baby brother, you're gon' lay me in my grave," she sighed. "Take this and dress your sorry self. Hurry! We leave in two minutes."

But then in the midst of the snow she saw something else. She gasped. Just outside the window was a beautiful person dressed all in white as bright as the moon, looking straight back into Probity's eyes.

This person smiled, then opened the window on the tips of her fingers and said, *Come, Probity Jones. It's time to go.*

Probity could only stare. *Go where?* she whispered.

The person outside was as tall as the night. She had wings wider than the dawn with feathers more silent than snow. Her robes were silken, and over her shoulders she wore a shawl of the softest cashmere.

She bent down and kissed Probity in the center of her forehead. *Why, to the Christmas Pageant, of course*, she said.

Suddenly all the stars in heaven flew down, ten million angels the sizes of children. It was as if the whole sky were a great wheel turning and burning: the angels circled the hills and the night and the shepherds, singing, *Glory to God in the highest, and peace to the people with whom he is pleased!*

The shepherds leaped up and raised their hands, worshiping God.

"Probity! Probity!" That was her little brother Charles' voice.

So Probity Jones switched on the light and ran to the back door of the apartment. She unlocked the lock, took hold of the doorknob and threw the door wide open.

Charles ran straight into the room and grabbed his sister and danced and danced. "I did it! I did it!" he cried. "I said all the words. Oh, Probe, it was just as if you were there with me!"

Elfrieda and Carolyn came in with snow-glitter on their shoulders. "Girl, you should've heard that angel sing," they said. "It was the angel of heaven. It surely was."

But behind them all, still framed in the doorway, was Probity's mama, her eyes as bright as diamonds. She was staring hard at her daughter.

"Child, something happened here, didn't it?"

"Yes'm, it did," Probity said.

"Look at you, baby. Look at my girl in a bright new coat!"

Probity walked forward and pressed her head against her mama's stomach.

The woman knelt down and hugged her. "What, child?" she whispered. "What happened tonight?"

"Oh mama, the angel of the Lord came down and carried me off to Bethlehem, and Jesus was born, and I was there, and so was Charles talkin' so beautiful—and Elfrieda and Carolyn, too. And I got to tell the good news to the people. Me, Mama! Probity Jones—I was at the pageant! We were all there together!"

307

Probity wrapped the shining shawl around her Mama and herself.

"And this came from the Fear Not Angel," she said. "Oh, Mama, the angel gave me a piece of herself to keep forever and forevermore."